Hi, I'm JIMMY!

Like me, you probably noticed the world is run by adults.
But ask yourself: Who would do the best job
of making books that *kids* will love?
Yeah. **Kids!**

So that's how the idea of JIMMY books came to life.
We want every JIMMY book to be so good
that when you're finished, you'll say,
"PLEASE GIVE ME ANOTHER BOOK!"

Give this one a try and see if you agree.
(If not, you're probably an adult!)

JIMMY Patterson Books for Young Readers

JAMES PATTERSON PRESENTS
Sci-Fi Junior High by John Martin and Scott Seegert
Sci-Fi Junior High: Crash Landing by John Martin
and Scott Seegert
How to Be a Supervillain by Michael Fry
How to Be a Supervillain: Born to Be Good
by Michael Fry
How to Be a Supervillain: Bad Guys Finish First
by Michael Fry
The Unflushables by Ron Bates
Ernestine, Catastrophe Queen by Merrill Wyatt
Scouts by Shannon Greenland

THE MIDDLE SCHOOL SERIES BY
JAMES PATTERSON
Middle School: The Worst Years of My Life
Middle School: Get Me Out of Here!
Middle School: Big Fat Liar
*Middle School: How I Survived Bullies, Broccoli,
and Snake Hill*
Middle School: Ultimate Showdown
Middle School: Save Rafe!
Middle School: Just My Rotten Luck
Middle School: Dog's Best Friend
Middle School: Escape to Australia
Middle School: From Hero to Zero
Middle School: Born to Rock
Middle School: Master of Disaster

THE I FUNNY SERIES BY JAMES PATTERSON
I Funny
I Even Funnier
I Totally Funniest
I Funny TV
I Funny: School of Laughs
The Nerdiest, Wimpiest, Dorkiest I Funny Ever

Big Words for Little Geniuses
Bigger Words for Little Geniuses
Cuddly Critters for Little Geniuses
The Candies Save Christmas

For exclusives, trailers, and other information,
visit jimmypatterson.org.

OL STORY

DOG DIARIES

MISSION IMPAWSIBLE

JAMES PATTERSON

WITH STEVEN BUTLER
ILLUSTRATED BY RICHARD WATSON

JIMMY Patterson Books
Little, Brown and Company
New York   Boston   London

JIMMY Patterson Books / Little, Brown and Company
Hachette Book Group
1290 Avenue of the Americas, New York, NY 10104

JamesPatterson.com

First North American edition: April 2020

Originally published in Great Britain by Penguin Random House UK, July 2019

JIMMY Patterson Books is an imprint of Little, Brown and Company, a division of Hachette Book Group, Inc. The Little, Brown name and logo are trademarks of Hachette Book Group, Inc. The JIMMY Patterson Books® name and logo are trademarks of JBP Business, LLC.

The publisher is not responsible for websites (or their content) that are not owned by the publisher.

The Hachette Speakers Bureau provides a wide range of authors for speaking events. To find out more, go to hachettespeakersbureau. com or call (866) 376-6591.

ISBN 978-0-316-49447-2

Library of Congress Control Number 2019957222

10 9 8 7 6 5 4 3 2 1

LSC-H

Printed in the United States of America

For Fran and Wilson
—S.B.

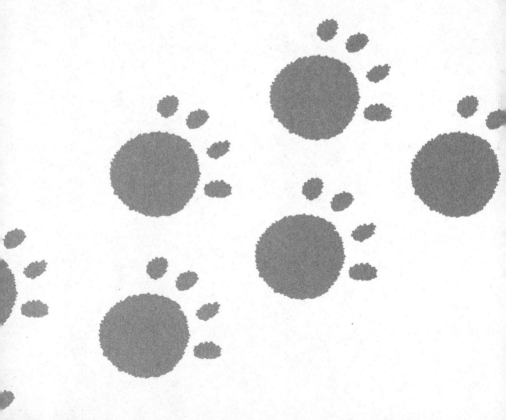

OH BOY! I knew it…I just knew it!
Only yesterday I was telling my best
pooch-pals, Odin
and Diego, that I'd
sniffed the hap-
hap-HAPPIEST
whiff of human on
the breeze and
now HERE YOU
ARE! A HUMAN!

Smells like…
HUGS and
MISCHIEF!

I can't tell you how exciting it is to know you're holding book three of my Dog Diaries in your five fingery digits, and we're about to go on ANOTHER adventure together...and this one's a humdinger!

A lot has happened since I wrote my last diary, and you won't believe what's been going on in the Catch-A-Doggy-Bone kennel lately.

But wait! What am I saying? I'm getting way too excited and scampering off ahead of myself.

What if we've never met before and you haven't read any of my stories? That's a terrible thought, but what if you HAVEN'T!?! Just think of all the fun and howl-tastic giggles you've missed out on.

Well, my person-pal, if that's the case and you know nothing about all the amazing things I've been up to since I came to live with my best-best-BESTEST pet human, Ruff, there's only one thing for it. I'll fill you in with all the details quicker than you can shout "THERE'S A RACCOON IN THE BACKYARD! LET'S GET IT!" and you'll be living a more poochified life in no time. I promise! And who wouldn't want to live like us masterful mutts, huh?

Okay…where do I start? Ummm…oh yeah! In case we haven't met before, my name is Junior. HELLO!

Junior Catch-A-Doggy-Bone, to be precise.

Only last year I came to stay with my new family and it has made me happier than a terrier with a tennis ball.

It's true!! Just the thought of that TERRIFIC day when Mom-Lady collected me and brought me back here to make a fresh start at kennel life makes my tail go CRAZY. I've got the urge to perform a Happy Dance right now, but don't worry, I won't, or we'll be here all day. Once I get started I can't stop for ages, and there's far too much catching up to do for me to be wasting time with yippin' and yappin' about.

First things first—you gotta meet my pet human. He's the GREATEST! Just look at him! Have you ever seen a more wonderful face?

4

RAFE KHATCHADORIAN

Ruff Catch-A-Doggy-Bone
x

I swear, my furless friend, I've never loved anyone or anything more in my whole life. Yep! Ruff is the most slobber-licious human in the whole of Hills Village and beyond. He's even better than my favorite stick!

We've already had some TREMENDOUS adventures together, shared some BARK-TASTIC feasts in the Food Room, and taught a few grizzly grown-ups and their pampered poodle-princesses that obedience and rules aren't for everyone. OH BOY, have we had some fun doing it!

But, before I spend all day yowling and howling on about my family-pack, there's something else I'm just DYING to tell you. It's more exciting than the time I found a whole bag of Canine Crispy Crackers under a bench at the dog park and I don't think I can keep it to myself for one more second, my furless friend.

Wanna hear? Ha ha! OF COURSE YOU DO!

All right, my person-pal. Brace yourself, because what I'm about to tell you will make you run around in circles, howling and drooling with joy.

DRUM ROLL, PLEASE!!!

Ruff and I…we're…we're…

AAAGH!! I can hardly get the words out!

Come on, Junior, you can do this!

Breathe in…

Breathe out…

Breathe in…

Breathe out…

Phew…that's better.

Okay, Junior. Tell the story properly and start at the beginning. Here goes…

It all started just last week…c'mon…

Last Tuesday

3:37 p.m.

So far, it had been a totally normal day, my person-pal.

Ruff and his little sister, Jawjaw, headed off for a day at school and I took Mom-Lady out for a walk on the end of my leash. She loves coming along with me on my usual jaunt to the dog park for a run-snuffle-bark-about with my best pooch-pals…

They're the greatest pooch-pals a dog like me could ever ask for, but I'll tell you more about those guys later, don't you worry.

BETTY

DIEGO

GENGHIS

LOLA

ODIN

After we got back from an AMAZING morning in the park (Lola found a half-eaten hamburger in a trash can! IT WAS EPIC!), I'd set about doing my very important daily routine...

Sniffing for new smells in all the corners of the kennel...

Growling at the hallway closet door to warn my archest of enemies, THE VACUUM CLEANER, to stay in there…

Snoozing in the sun on the Picture Box Room rug…

Howling at the mailman. HE LOVES IT WHEN I DO THAT!

Barking at raccoons in the backyard...

So…by the time I'd finished my list of daily chores and the afternoon arrived, I was content and curled up on the comfy squishy thing, minding my own business and chewing on a particularly tasty sock from Jawjaw's room…

Oh, wait…in case you haven't met Ruff's super-sneery little sister, Jawjaw, before. This is her…

~~GEORGIA~~
Jawjaw

Now, I'm not supposed to go in Jawjaw's Sleep Room anymore. She's been mega mad at me ever since I stole one of her creepy little plastic humans and…well…maybe cooked it a little bit—but it wasn't my fault!

It felt awful being told I was a BA…BAD…
BAD DO…Oh, you know what I'm trying to
say. Those are terrible words to a mutt's ears.
HORRIBLE!

I knew I wasn't supposed to be in Jawjaw's Sleep Room, but I couldn't help myself.
You see, things from Jawjaw's room taste
SOOOOOO delicious. Mainly because
I'm forbidden from eating them. It's a real
conundrum. The things you know you aren't
allowed to chew on are always the yummi-
est, and Jawjaw's creepy little humans taste
like dust and dirt and plastic. SCRUM-A-
LUMPTIOUS, if you ask me!

But a little while ago, Ruff and I had to take
obedience classes (YUCK! I HATE THOSE
TWO WORDS ALMOST AS MUCH AS BAD
DOOO…Agh! Forget it!) and I'm trying my

best to keep us both out of trouble by being a perfect pooch. These days I have to make do with enjoying the occasional sock that I can sneak from Jawjaw's laundry pile, right by her door...and enjoying it I was.

It was such a tasty snack that I almost completely failed to notice something terrific was about to happen...something completely wonderful!

RUFF WAS COMING HOME FROM SCHOOL!!

I swear it's one of the best-best-BEST parts of the day, my furless friend. Nothing fills my houndy heart and makes me Happy-Dance like the moment my perfect pet human comes home from a long day at Hills Village Middle School.

There are very strict rules for the moment when a dog's best friend gets home after classes, and you should definitely know what they are. I take poochy pride in sticking to these exactly…

RULES FOR WHEN RUFF GETS HOME:

1. When you hear the big yellow moving people-box on wheels stop in the street, you must:

2. Bound over the comfy squishy thing and clamber onto the window ledge

3. Wedge your face against the glass to make sure you can really, really see your human getting off the big yellow moving people-box on wheels

4. Bark as loudly as possible until your pet human looks up at you from the sidewalk outside your kennel

5. Once they've seen you in the window, leap off the window ledge and sprint as quickly as your four paws can carry you

out of the Picture Box Room and into the hallway

6. Once you're in the hallway, run to the front door and sit as close to it as you can possibly get

7. Wag your tail slowly while you wait to hear their footsteps outside

8. Once you hear your person-pal on the front step, accelerate your tail wags to HAPPY DANCE SPEED

9. When the front door opens, BEGIN HAPPY DANCE! It is EXTREMELY IMPORTANT that your dance includes jumping, spinning, nipping, yapping, licking, clambering, barking, howling, slobbering, whining, and…maybe a little bit of peeing and pooping for extra flair.

3:57 p.m.

Phewy! That was one long Happy Dance. As I was saying before I got distracted, Jawjaw's sock was such a tasty tidbit that I completely missed rules 1 to 7!! Can you believe it?! It wasn't until Ruff's jangle-keys clicked in the front door that I realized he was home, so I treated him to a seriously long and extra yap-a-licious

"THE HOP AND TWIST"

"THE POKEY PATS"

performance
to make up for
only doing half
a welcome.

"THE DROP AND DROOL"

Ruff was so impressed, let me tell you. It makes him SOOOOOO HAPPY when I leave paw-prints all over the front of his jeans. It's his favorite!

Anyway…after my show-stopping routine, Ruff and I set straight off to snuggle up in front of the picture box and watch an episode of *LAW PAWS*!

It's the BEST cop show, all about a detective and his canine sidekick who solve terrible crimes and mysteries together. I LOVE watching these moving pictures with Ruff and they're the reason my understanding of the Peoplish language is getting so good. I can recognize most words nowadays, but my fellow Catch-A-Doggy-Bone pack don't know that…HA HA!

THAT'S HOW I FOUND OUT ABOUT THE EXCITING NEWS!!

4:25 p.m.

Mom-Lady walked into the Picture Box Room and said it! SHE JUST SAID IT!! She poked her head through the door and, without any clue that I know what she's talking about, came out with...

RAFE, DON'T FORGET YOU NEED TO PACK A BAG FOR THE VACATION. YOU CAN'T GO TO HOLLYWOOD IN JEANS AND A SWEATSHIRT! AND PACK UP JUNIOR'S THINGS TOO...

AAAAAAAAAAAAAAAAAGGG GGGGHHHHHHH!!!!

Can you imagine it, my furless friend? Me, Junior, going to HOLLYWOOD!! Whoever would have thought that a mangy mutt like me would be heading to a shiny place like that ON VACATION?!!

What did I tell you, my person-pal? Have you ever heard anything more waggy-tail-icious in your life? I didn't think so. Never in all my dog years have I gone on a trip with my pet human before, and I am itching with delight...or fleas...or BOTH! Who knows? But one thing's for sure: I AM SO THRILLED I COULD PEE ON EVERY RUG AROUND THE KENNEL FOR A MONTH!

Ruff doesn't know that I'm on to him yet. That sneaky-sneaker thinks he's going to surprise me on the day, but you can't pull the leash over my eyes. No sireeee! They don't call me "SHERLOCK BONES, THE SUPER SLEUTH" for nothing!

Okay…nobody calls me that. But they would if they knew how great I am at sniffing out secrets.

Now, my furless friend, you may be wondering why I'm so excited. You may also be scratching your little human head, saying, "HOW DOES JUNIOR EVEN KNOW WHAT HOLLYWOOD IS?"

Well, you may not be aware of this, but I'm practically an expert on HOLLYWOOD! I'll explain why…

Back before I was the happiest hound on the planet, living with the Catch-A-Doggy-Bone pack, I spent my days behind bars. I'm not proud of it, my person-pal, but I was a pooch prison pup!

It's the stuff of nightmares. I've never seen a scarier, lonelier, more BONE-JANGLING place in my life. It's where I met my pooch-pals, and we spent our days all sad and miserable in a cage without so much as a tummy-rub, nose-boop, or even the occasional treat.

I bet I know what you're thinking...I bet you're reading this with tears streaming down your furless face. Your brain will be racing and you'll be yelling...

THIS IS YOU

You'd be right to wonder that, my person-pal. Sometimes I feel amazed that we all coped in such a horrifying place, and I'm not sure we would have if it hadn't been for an ancient scruffy chow chow in the cell next to ours.

OLD MAMA MANGE

Crimes:

Pooping in public
Gnawing on benches

Howling at police officers
Stealing sandwiches
Petrifying pigeons

That farty old fiend would stay awake long into the night telling us stories through the bars about her INCREDIBLE life and all the places she'd visited, and one of her favorite stories that she loved to tell was all about her time in...you guessed it!

HOLLYWOOD!

Back in her youngly years, before she was old and mangy, Old Mama Mange spent her days in the sunniest city on earth, and if what she told us was true, she had a bark-tastic time!

I just can't believe that after hearing all those TERRIFIC tales about Hollywood in my dismal days at Hills Village Dog Shelter, Ruff and Mom-Lady are taking me to see it! This is going to be LICK-A-LICIOUS! And who knows? Maybe this is our chance to get famous and act in a moving picture like Mama Mange! NO! EVEN BETTER! Ruff and I could have our own cop drama! We could be megastars!

Just imagine it, my furless friend…

SIGH!

Back to today: the following Wednesday

10:26 a.m.

So...here we are, my furless friend. You've caught up with everything that's happened in the past week and the MASSIVE secret that I found out.

I'm not going to lie to you, it's been seriously tough trying to pretend I don't know about our vacation to HOLLYWOOD. My tail

has been on waggy overdrive all week and nearly given me away a few times!

I never thought I'd say this, but ever since Mom-Lady blurted out the secret I've spent every morning waiting for Ruff to go to school. Can you imagine something so crazy?! ME...wanting my marvelous pet human to go to school?!

Don't panic, I haven't gone loop-the-loop crazy or something. Nope! It's just that when Ruff's around I can't plan what essentials to pack, or what amazing things I want to see or do when we're out in the sausage-meat-paved paradise that is Hollywood.

Ruff and Jawjaw set off about an hour ago and Mom-Lady has gone to work, leaving me free to plot and decide exactly what needs to be done.

THINGS I NEED
FOR OUR TOP SECRET
VACATION:

• DOGGY BRUSH FOR
  FLUFF-A-LICIOUS FUR

• LEMON-SCENTED POOCH
  SHAMPOO FOR EXTRA WHIFF

• MY FANCY GREEN COLLAR
  FROM THE DANDY DOG SHOW

• MAP OF THE BEST PEE SPOTS
  IN HOLLYWOOD

• EXTRA TREATS FOR
  A MUTT ON THE GO

That ought to do it, I think. With these essentials I'm sure to be spotted and whisked into a moving picture with Ruff before you can shout "ACTION!"

Thursday

12:24 p.m.

I swear to you, my person-pal, I'm not actually sure I can handle all this waiting. I'm so excited, I could explode like a fluffy firework.

I've been snooping at breakfast-time when Ruff, Jawjaw, and Mom-Lady are sitting around the table eating their...what do you call it? Toost and scrumbled oggs? Don't ask me—I might be able to understand Peoplish words better than most mutts, but it doesn't mean I know everything.

Anyway…I've been pretending to have a snooze under the table while everyone else is snuffling their meals, and I've found out lots about the plans for our vacation.

Most of what I've heard is SUPER thrilling, but I'm afraid there's some not-so-good news too. According to Mom-Lady, we're not heading off on our BARK-TASTIC TRIP until Saturday. SATURDAY?!?! That's another two days away!

HOW AM I SUPPOSED TO WAIT THAT LONG?

This is going to be tough…

5:27 p.m.

Okay...I admit I may be getting a bit impatient, but what do you expect when I'm trying to pass the time before a vacation to HOLLY-WOOD?! It's unbearable! I've been hopping about like a springer spaniel! Get it? Ha!

What am I saying? This is no time for jokes!

Being the masterful mutt that I am, I've been whiling away the hours thinking lots and lots about all the exciting stuff Ruff and I are going to do. Then, before I knew it, a plan popped into my head that could change the lives of the Catch-A-Doggy-Bone pack forever!

It's simple really...

Old Mama Mange always said that it's easy to get famous in Hollywood. So why am I daydreaming about being in a cop show with my pet human, when I could become a MEGASTAR? I just wasn't thinking big enough!

Anyone who's ever met me knows I'm a super-good singer. I'M SERIOUS! No one could out-YOWL me back in pooch prison.

Instead of doing all the touristy things, like snuffling up the Sunset Strip or barking along the boulevards, I'm going to SING at the top of my voice wherever we go.

I'll be discovered by one of those funny talenty folks I've seen on the picture box in a jiffy.

Who could resist my amazing voice, huh?
In no time I'll be bigger than...than...than
Justin Bie-BARK...or Lady GRRR-GRRR...or
Ariana GRUNTY!

46

Just picture it, my person-pal. Close your eyes and imagine how TERRIFIC it will be once I'm a world-famous singing sensation. My face would be on EVERY picture-box program, and I'll be so rich, I could buy a lifetime supply of Meaty-Giblet-Jumble-Chum and have an entire room filled with Canine Crispy Crackers. I'll only chew on the best-BEST-BESTEST sticks, and I'd build the biggest kennel-castle in Hills Village for all my pack and pooch-pals to live in...Oh! I've thought real hard about this part. It'll be the grandest, most lick-a-licious, MOST

HOWL-A-RIFIC building you've ever clapped your person-peepers on, my furless friend. The new home I'm planning will be a towering treat-fest...a palatial pooch park...A SKY-SCRAPING SNACK SHACK!

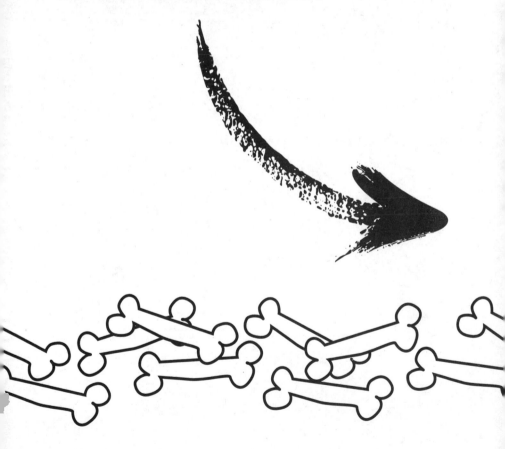

Howling platform

Grass Carpets

Swimming Pool filled with Doggo-Drops

Vending machine filled with the best sticks

Giant telescope for spying on RACCOONS!
Ruff's sleep room
Ensuite peeing spot
Barky ball room
Yard for pooping

It'll be the envy of every dog in Hills Village, especially the snooty ones who live in the fancy kennels over on the far side of town. Pampered princesses like Duchess the poodle and her HORRIBLE pet human, Iona Stricker, will turn green with jealousy. Ha!

SMELLS LIKE BOREDOM

EVIL EYES

DEVIOUS KNEES

IONA STRICKER

DUCHESS

While my pooch-pals and I are enjoying a poochified pool party and a dip in the Doggo-Drops, they'll be wishing they'd been just a little friendlier back when we were in OBEDI-ENCE CLASSES!

It's going to be FANTASTIC, my furless friend. There's no way my plan will fail, I just know it! We'll be living in my MUTT-MANSION in no time.

Now all I have to do is keep calm and wait until Saturday. The trick is to keep my mind busy, I think.

Hmmmm...I'm going to go see how Ruff is doing...He's in his Sleep Room doing his homework, and I know he loves it when I climb up and leave paw-marks on it.

Friday

10:26 a.m.

AAAAAAAAAAAAAAAAAAAAGGGGG-
HHHHHHHHH!!!!

I can't...I can't...I...I...I think my tail is going to fly off like a helicopter...I...I'm...SO EXCITED!

You won't believe what I'm about to tell you, my person-pal. Just when you thought that things couldn't get any more HUMDING-ERISH than knowing I'm going to Hollywood to become a MEGASTAR...I've just found out something EVEN BETTER!

You're going to YIP when you hear this, my furless friend. You'll be howling at the moon in delight for weeks to come when I tell you.

Are you ready?

Are you sure?

Okay...here goes!!

MY POOCH-PALS ARE ALL COMING ON VACATION TOO!

I...I...can't believe it. What was already

going to be a BRILLIANT trip away with my Catch-A-Doggy-Bone pack has now turned into the GREATEST DOGGY ESCAPE to the sunshine and beaches and sausage-meat streets of my dreams!

Here's how I found out…

Ruff and Jawjaw were at school…again— those poor things—and Mom-Lady dropped me off at the kennel of my best pooch-pals, Odin and Diego, while she went to work.

I LOVE visiting their home. It smells so different to our kennel and there are so many new things to taste and tear and play with when you haven't been there for a while.

Anyway, we were out in the backyard, sniffing for RACCOONS, when I knew I just had to tell them about the GINORMOUS secret I was on to.

For a second they both looked shocked, but then they kinda smirked. I'm not sure how I was expecting my furry friends to react, but a little bit impressed would have been good. After all, it's not every day a dog promises to build a pooch palace with a room just for pooping!

But, just when I was about to ask if they'd heard me correctly, Diego threw back his head and howled...

I just couldn't believe it. All three of us Happy-Danced all over their backyard.

MI AMIGO! SO ARE WE!!
WE DIDN'T THINK ANYONE ELSE WAS GOING AND WE'VE BEEN KEEPING THE SECRET FOR DAYS!

Then Odin had a BRILLIANT idea: "Let's go tell the rest of the pooch-pack. Maybe they're coming to Hollywood too!"

That would be too good to be true! We just HAD to find out, right that moment. So, when Odin and Diego's pet human was busy folding laundry, Diego climbed onto my back and I clambered onto Odin's. Then in one big leap, Odin jumped up onto the top of the lumber pile near the trash cans.

From there we could see over the fence to the rest of the neighborhood down the hill, and I did a little investigative barking—investi-barking...

Now, just like you humans and your Peoplish language, us mutts are masters of canine communication. Our language is Doglish and there really is no language in the world that's more beautiful.

I'm not kidding.

Doglish is FABULOUS and super useful to learn. I bet you don't even know these easy phrases...

"OOOOHW-OOOOHW-WUH-OOOOOOOOOOHW" means "I'm hungry."

"GRRR-GUH-WAHOOOOOOOOOH" means "I wanna go outside."

"BROOOOAAAHHH" means "Scratch my tummy, please."

"RUH" means "There's a RACCOON out in the trash and it looked at me and I really think I should go bark at it and maybe sniff it for a little while to make sure everything is safe."

Anyway...after a bit of loud howling, it didn't take long to contact the rest of my pack—Lola, Betty, and Genghis.

5:37 p.m.

I never imagined such a happy moment in all my little life, my person-pal. After lots of yapping and yowling back and forth, it turns out all the pet humans of our neighborhood have planned a mass vacation. We're all traveling together and I can't wait!

Ever since I got back here to the Catch-A-Doggy-Bone kennel, I've been skipping around on cloud nine…err…cloud canine…

6:22 p.m.

Eeee! It's all getting so close! Mom-Lady is sprinting about the house yelling and shouting orders, while Jawjaw and Ruff are busily packing their bags ready for tomorrow.

It makes my houndy heart warmer than a pack of puppies piled up in a cuddle-puddle to know that all across the town, my pooch-pals and their human pets are stuffing their belongings into cases and preparing to head off on the trip of a lifetime.

I could cry with joy!

9 p.m.

Well, that's it, my furless friend. We're ready to go....

The cases are packed, Mom-Lady has gone to bed, Jawjaw is reading her sightseeing map for the best places to visit, and Ruff and I are curled up on his bed.

I swear I've never felt this happy and content in my life. Ruff has even packed a special little bag just for me, with a few treats and my doggy food bowl in it. He's the best!

I'm just going to let him work on his drawings and drift off for a good sleep before the big day. Things couldn't get any better than this...

Saturday

9:47 a.m.

STOP
EVERYTHING

I…I…I can't breathe! I can't think!

It's…it's all gone wrong, my person-pal! I…I…I

can't get the words out! I feel like the whole world is spinning and my paws have turned to jelly.

I...I'll try to tell you what happened, but I'm not sure I even know myself!

CALM DOWN, JUNIOR! Think of treats, and tennis balls, and the dog park...Okay...

Ev...ev...everything seemed great this morning...

I woke up and did my daily lap of the kennel, treading on everyone's forehead to wake them up.

So...we were up and all very excited. Mom-Lady made a quick breakfast of oggs and piggy strips on wifflies...

I had my usual bowl of Crunchy-Lumps.

OGGS

PIGGY STRIPS

WIFFLIES

Then, once everyone had visited the Rainy Poop Room and got dressed, Ruff and Mom-Lady grabbed all the bags and we headed out into the front yard.

It was the most wonderful sight, my person-pal. All my pooch-pals and their pet humans were on the sidewalk and there was a huge moving people-box on wheels parked in the street. It wasn't like the normal kind that you see rattling by at all hours, though. No, this one was gigantic!

At first, everything seemed completely fine, and exciting, and noisy, bustly, and exactly the way it should feel on the morning of the best vacation of our lives. But then…I noticed that all the cases had been loaded into the stupendous moving people-box on wheels except for the little bags containing our doggy stuff. They were all left on the sidewalk, and our humans all seemed to be waiting for something.

Mom-Lady kept checking her watch and grunting, saying something like...

DOG GUYS?! Who were the dog guys?!

We didn't have to wait long to find out, my person-pal. Just when I was getting more confused than a Rottweiler on a roller coaster, a battered old moving people-box called a truck (I know this from the mailman and the garbage people) trundled round the corner and parked up alongside us.

It's all such a blur, my furless friend. Before we could run away, or bark, or play dead, our pet humans loaded us into the back of the truck. My heart was racing faster than a greyhound and I couldn't tell why Mom-Lady and Ruff kept smiling.

And that's when all my worst fears came true.

We...we're not going to Hollywood with our humans! They're sending us away!

NOOOOOOOOOOOOOOOOOOOOOOO!!!!

9:49 a.m.

THIS IS THE WORST MOMENT OF MY LIFE!!!

The men in the front of the truck started the engine and we're driving off. I can still see Ruff waving from the sidewalk! Maybe if I use my best "DON'T LEAVE ME!" howl, he'll change his mind…

This is horrible, my furless friend! I feel like my heart might break! How could my Catch-A-Doggy-Bone pack send me away while they're having fun and frolics around Hollywood without me?

Is this because I cooked Jawjaw's creepy little plastic human?

Is it because I snaffled a turkey leg from last Fangs Giving and stashed it in Mom-Lady's walking shoes for safekeeping? No...it can't be! She hasn't found it yet!

WHY IS THIS HAPPENING???

10:07 a.m.

This truck has been driving for ages and it's showing no signs of stopping. We drove all the way past the Dandy-Dog store and the gates to the dog park. I've never even traveled this far!! Who knows what horrors await us and...what if...what if...? I can't even say it!

What if we're being sent back to the Hills Village Dog Shelter?! I don't ever want to go back there—I'm certain I'd never survive it. That pooch prison was a treatless, tummy-tickle-less TERROR!

One thing's for sure: If this rattly and rusty truck takes us back to Hills Village Dog Shelter, I'm a goner. I'll be a dead dog in no time! A drool ghoul! Franken-Junior!!

I won't last a day—no, scratch that—
an hour—scratch that—a SECOND in that
dreadful place. Even the thought of it makes
my fur bristle with fear!

Everyone back here in the truck is in a state of shock and it's getting real ugly, let me tell you. Odin is slobbering like a St Bernard at a barbecue, Lola can't stop crying, Betty is howling, Diego has curled into a ball and won't unravel, and Genghis peed in the corner...so...no one wants to sit over there just now.

What are we going to do, my person-pal?!

10:10 a.m.

Okay...so I have one piece of good news. Just when we were all about to give up and sink into doggy despair, Betty found a scrap of paper screwed up in a corner of the truck—not the one Genghis peed in, don't panic—and it turns out we're definitely not heading to Hills Village Dog Shelter.

Using my excellent understanding of the Peoplish language, I managed to read a few words here and there, and it seems our pet humans have booked us into Barking Meadows Care Retreat.

And, judging by this flyer, maybe it won't be so bad after all...

Shower your pet
with love and affection
by checking them into
BARKING
MEADOWS
THIS DOGGY DESTINATION
IS THE CENTER OF
RELAXATION AND WELL-BEING
FOR OUR FOUR-LEGGED FRIENDS.
HERE THEY CAN ENJOY TREATS
AND TUMMY TICKLES A'PLENTY.

Ha! What was I worrying about, my person-pal? Okay…I'm not going to Hollywood with Ruff, which makes me feel super sad, but if Barking Meadows is as pampery and luxurious as this flyer says it is, I have a feeling we won't be having such a bad time after all. I'll keep you posted…

10:17 a.m.

This place is...is...well...IT'S FANTASTIC!

The truck just parked up in front of one of the grandest buildings I've ever seen. Then we were all let out and led inside and...it's SO CLEAN!!

I swear to you, my person-pal. Even if I take a really big sniff, I can't detect even the tiniest whiff of dirt, and my nose can snuffle out anything! MOM-LADY WOULD LOVE IT HERE!!

10:31 a.m.

Ha ha! We've each just been given brand-new red leather collars for our stay, and one of the guys from the truck (the one who smells like soap and shoe polish) has clipped a super-soft leash to each of them. It looks like we're going on a walk around the place to figure out where everything

is and smell everything there is to smell.
BRILLIANT! LET'S GO!!

12:08 p.m.

HOLLYWOOD/SCHMOLLYWOOD!!! I can't believe I thought I was a goner back there in that truck, my person-pal. This place is far better than a city with sausage-meat sidewalks! I almost feel sad for Ruff, Jawjaw, and Mom-Lady that they're missing it.

The oldy-baldy guy from the truck—his name is George...I heard one of the other humans say so—led us around the building and showed us so many AMAZING THINGS. He even spoke to us like we were humans! Not a bit of baby-talk or barky-ordery-moany-ness at all!

I just can't believe my eyes, my furless friend! But mostly I can't believe my ears! There are squillions of other dogs here, but it's so quiet! They must all be completely peacefully pampered. I guess they've all been for a visit to the SPANIEL SPA. I can't wait to go and try out some of the TREAT-ments. We just walked past and I caught a glimpse of all the amazing things they offer.

Get a load of this!!

SPA TREATMENTS

—⸙—

PAW PAMPERING
WHISKER PERMING
TAIL TRIMMING
NOSE SHINING
NAIL CLIPPING
TUMMY TICKLING
CHIN WAXING
EAR TUSSLING

12:15 p.m.

Today has certainly been a strange one, my person-pal. I can't believe it's only midday and already I thought I was going on the greatest vacation in the history of vacations, then thought I was going to shrivel up and die with fear and boredom at Hills Village Dog Shelter, and now I've been paraded around the most incredible doggy retreat I've ever seen...EVER!

Ruff and Mom-Lady certainly know how to delight a dog, that's for sure.

George just showed me and the pooch-pack to our room and it couldn't be farther from that cold cage back in doggy prison. We're all staying in a kind of pen that's filled with cushions and blankets and smells like sleepy time and morning breath…two of my favorite scents!

Well, I guess that's me sorted for the next forty-five minutes. After all the excitement we've had this morning, I'm going to catch a little beauty sleep. I want to look pooch-er-ific for when we all head down to lunch and meet the other dog guests in this swanky place. See you in a little bit, my person-pal.

12:58 p.m.

OH, WOW! I wish you could be here, I really do. The Food Room is so big, you could fit the whole of the Catch-A-Doggy-Bone kennel inside it. I've never seen a ceiling so high before…except for the sky!

There are rows upon rows of gleaming gold dog bowls lined up along the floor and all of the canine customers are wandering in and sitting down next to theirs…it's still very quiet though. No one seems to be making a sound at all.

12:59 p.m.

Huh! Well, so much for meeting the other dog guests, my furless friend. These pooches are rude! No one wants to speak. I've tried several times, but each dog just stares at me with wide eyes.

Something weird is going on, I swear it. Since when does a mutt meet a new potential pooch-pal and not go sniff its butt or roll over and show its belly? This is very confusing!

1 p.m.

Oh no! Oh no! Oh no!

I don't think I can take any more surprises, my person-pal. Now I know why the other dogs were acting strange and didn't want to talk when I asked them about food.

George and a whole bunch of his human coworkers just came out with our special lunches and placed them down in our bowls. For a tiny second I was confused by the strange smells coming from them...sort of like mud and sadness and poop, until I realized...the bowl was filled with...

VEGETABLES

This can't be right! Who would ever be so evil to make a hungry hound eat carrots and celery? This is inhuman! It's unthinkable! It's horrific! Ruff and Mom-Lady have sent me and my pooch-pals on a VEGETABLE VACATION!!!

10 p.m.

Psssst…it's me…Junior!

I'm pretty sure you must have run screaming from the room, or thrown this book under your bed, or dived headfirst into the laundry pile after you read the last few pages. But it's okay…If you keep quiet, it's safe to come out, my person-pal.

If you're anything like me and my mutt-mates, you'll probably be very shaken and wondering if the whole world has gone loop-the-loop crazy.

No wonder all those miserable pooches were so quiet. What kind of mutt would want to happily yap, or brightly bark, or snuffly sniff a new dog's butt, when they've only had vegetables to eat? It's like one of the scary moving pictures I watched on the picture box with Ruff!

Where were the chicken chunks? Where were the turkey twists or the beefy bites?

WHERE WAS THE MEATY-GIBLET-JUMBLE-CHUM?!

None of my pooch-pack ate a single mouthful of that terrible food…and when we were finally allowed to go off and explore the Spaniel Spa and bubbling pooch pool, we were all too sad to try anything.

This is worse than being called a…a… BAD DOG!! I can't even bring myself to wag my tail…

By the time dinner came around we were all practically starving, but that meal was even worse! For dinner, the Barking Meadows staff served us lentils and Brussels sprouts! It was terrifying!

Lola panicked with hunger when she saw what we'd been given and started gobbling mouthfuls of the little cabbage balls!

Can you imagine it? A respectable pooch like Lola, forced to eat RABBIT FOOD! If dogs could turn green, I swear she would have at that moment, and now she has serious wind…even for a French bulldog! Poor little Diego was walking behind her, minding his own business, when she let rip and launched him into the air like a tiny canine comet!

It was awful!

He's having to sleep under his pillow tonight, instead of on top of it…y'know…for safety.

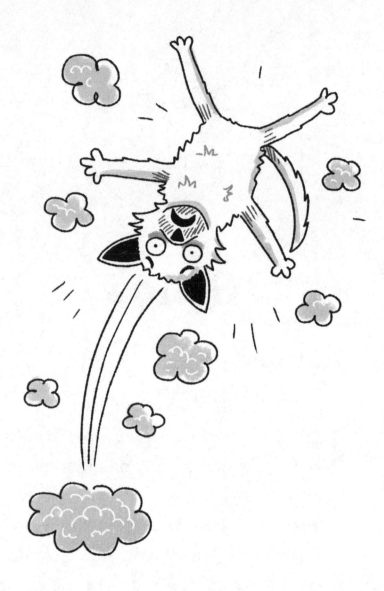

Sunday

7:30 a.m.

Ugh! This is even more dreadful than I thought, my person-pal. I barely got a moment of sleep!

Y'see, the great big Sleep Room with all the doggy-pens might be super comforta-ble and filled with the most snooze-a-licious blankets and cushions, but every pooch in there was howling like a hungry werewolf for the entire night.

It seems everyone was having bad dreams…

By the time I finally dropped off to sleep it was after 3 a.m., and I was soon having the most gut-wrenching nightmare too! It was a howl-o-rific screamer about being chased by a giant stick of gnashing celery! At first I thought it wanted to eat me…but then I realized: It wanted me to EAT IT!!

Ugh!

8 a.m.

Okay, my furless friend. We've been summoned for breakfast. Oldy-baldy George came in and dinged a little bell and now we're all shuffling off to the Food Room. I'm not going to lie...I've never felt so jittery. Never in my whole life have I been nervous about being fed.

I can't believe Ruff would do this to me. It's one thing for him to send me—ME, his best, BEST, BESTEST pal in the whole world—to a dog retreat while he goes off to Hollywood, but how could he send me to a place that feeds salad to dogs?

Don't get me wrong...I know there are plenty of humans who love to gorge on greens, and that's fine. But to a dog, THIS IS TORTURE!

8:07 a.m.

I can't cope, my person-pal. My paws are trembling...my belly is gurgling...my nose is dry! If the staff here at Barking Meadows bring out bowls of carrots and lettuce for breakfast, I'm not going to make it. I can feel my life slipping away. Twenty-four hours without the meaty loveliness of dog treats has done strange things to me. Even now I swear I'm seeing things...

8:08 a.m.

Here they come...all those staff-type humans with our morning meal. Please let it be Canine Crispy Crackers! Please let it be Canine Crispy Crackers! PLEASE LET IT BE CANINE CRISPY CRACKERS!!!

8:09 a.m.

NOOOOOOOOOOOOOOOOOOOOOOOO!!!!

GOODBYE, CRUEL WORLD! If you ever find this book, please tell my Catch-A-Doggy-Bone pack that I loved them, and I don't blame them (MUCH) for sending me off to this terrible place to slowly turn into a vegetable-shriveled husk.

Muesli?! I can't eat MUESLI! What part of a turkey does muesli come from?

And SPINACH?!?!?! I don't even know what that is, but it's green. BLEEEUUUUUGGH!!

This is the end! I know it—any minute now I'll be gone! Suffocated by the stinksome whiff of too much broccoli!

8:10 a.m.

Any minute now…Farewell, my furless friend. It was wonderful knowing you.

8:11 a.m.

Any minute now…

8:12 a.m.

Nearly there…

8:13 a.m.

Hmmm…Why am I still here?

Okay, so maybe broccoli isn't going to kill me, but I can't put up with much more of this. Every pooch in this parsnip palace is completely miserable!

Yesterday at dinner I saw a bloodhound eating parsley puffs. PARSLEY PUFFS!! That's what old George and his grinning, preening cronies have been handing out as treats! Surely that's criminal!?! They should all be thrown in jail!!

10:27 a.m.

We're all out on the lawn with a man they call Bob—he was the other guy in the truck yesterday—and a lady called Patty. They keep throwing tennis balls for us to chase after but no one's in the mood. Not even Odin, and he's a champion at playing fetch!

11:43 a.m.

I tried to cheer myself up with a trip to the Spaniel Spa to get my tail curled, but no matter how hard the spa-guy tried, it just kept drooping.

1 p.m.

Lunch has just been served...It's braised lettuce with string beans, my person-pal, and the most terrible thing happened when George put it down in front of me. I'm a little ashamed to say this, but for the briefest of seconds...I...I...I was tempted to try it!!

WHAT'S HAPPENING TO ME!?!

The SNACK MASTER, the TERROR OF THE TREAT CUPBOARD, the SUPER SCARFER OF SAUSAGES...wanted to eat string beans!! At this rate, I'll soon be one of those silent staring dogs who shuffle around Barking Meadows. By the time Ruff and Mom-Lady come to collect me, I'll be a vegetable-zombie! A VOMBIE!!!

8:57 p.m.

Check, check...This is Special Agent Junior reporting for duty.

Can you keep a secret, my furless friend? What am I saying?! Of course you can!

Okay, don't tell anyone, but my pooch-pack are going to escape from this place. We have to!!

A few hours ago, we had another howl-o-rific and slightly painful incident at dinner. When Betty took one look at the asparagus soup they served us, she got all confused and wobbly and thought Odin's back leg was a great big chicken drumstick. Before we could stop her, she darted behind the big fella and tried to gnaw on his enormous fluffy rump.

It was Howl Central!

It was in that moment we all knew what had to be done. We can't wait around this salady shack for a second longer.

Tonight, when all the other canine customers are asleep and howling through their veggie-mares, we're going to have a SUPER-SECRET pack meeting and cook up a plan to get out of here and back to Hills Village.

I'll let you know how it goes...

Midnight

Monday

6:21 a.m.

TODAY'S THE DAY, MY PERSON-PAL! We stayed up talking long into the night and we've come up with lots of terrific plans to get out of this cauliflower castle once and for all. One of them has to work...I just know it...we only have to wait until the coast is clear after breakfast...

9:42 a.m.

BLEEUURRGH! Well, I'm glad that's over with. George, Bob, and Patty just tried to serve us pumpkin parcels with turnip trifle. GROSS!!!

What I wouldn't do for a tiny piece of Mom-Lady's steak surprise that she cooks on special occasions. Sigh! I miss my Catch-A-Doggy-Bone pack…BUT…I don't have time to think about that right now.

Breakfast is over, which means we have a few hours to try to escape from this mush-room mansion. Here goes…

There's no way this will fail. It's foolproof!

OPERATION DIG FOR DEAR LIFE!

10:02 a.m.

Hmmmm…that didn't quite go to plan.
I think we got a bit lost…

10:05 a.m.

Never mind! We've got loads of other BARK-TASTIC ideas…

The first idea might have failed, but there's NO WAY this one will. FREEDOM, HERE WE COME!

11:26 a.m.

GUH!!! Well, that wasn't a success. We couldn't get our paws on any Brussels sprouts, but Odin managed to sneak a load of turnips from this morning's breakfast. At first it looked as though we might just have lift-off with the help of our farty friend's amazing powers...

…but it turns out turnips aren't nearly as powerful as sprouts.

We had a watery landing…

12:37 p.m.

Don't despair, my person-pal. We...errr... we'll keep trying. I know...well...I think...we can do this...

Hmmm…on second thought, that one may not be such a great idea. None of us knows our addresses, and what if we get sent to the wrong place? We could end up being delivered to Carrot-zona, Oklaho-marrow, Tex-asparagus, or Las Vegan!!!

How about…

Maybe not. I know I'm a genius pooch, but those pedals look tricky...and what's the turny wheely thing at the front for? It seems important.

UGH! There's got to be a way for us to get out of Barking Meadows.

Think, Junior, think!

3:36 p.m.

I've got it, my person-pal! I TOLD YOU I'M A GENIUS POOCH!!
    After a disgusting lunch of pimento pastries and a failed attempt at shimmying along the washing line at the back of the building where they dry the staff's uniforms...

…I was feeling sadder than a basset hound who's lost his bark, so I plodded off to the bushes at the far end of the ball lawn for a peaceful poop, all by myself. Ever since I was a tiny pup, I've found I always get my absolute bestest ideas whenever I'm having a quiet moment doing…well…you know…

AND GUESS WHAT?!

PEACEFUL-POOP-TIME DIDN'T FAIL ME!!

The answer to getting out of Barking Meadows has been right in front of our noses all along. I can't believe I didn't see it before!

The only way we're going to make it out of this healthy hazard-zone is to get every single pooch on the premises to pitch in and help. If we can work like one BIG pack there may be a teensy-weensy chance that all of us—AND I MEAN ALL OF US—can escape this miserable place.

I've called an ALL-MUTT meeting by the jungle gym at four o'clock. That's when George,

Bob, Patty, and the rest of the Barking Meadows staff head off to the Back Room to prepare all the vile veggies for our evening meal, so it's the perfect time to rally the troops.

It's not going to be easy to break the vombies out of their tomato-trances but I've prepared a speech and everything. Now I just need to hope that everyone shows up…

4:25 p.m.

Oh, sometimes I don't know why I bother!

The moment was perfectly planned! The humans were all distracted! My speech was EPIC!!

I'm not even exaggerating when I say my speech was worthy of a big sparkly award, my person-pal, but guess what—all those unhappy hounds and tortured terriers said…

Not one of the pooches in the crowd had the GET-UP-AND-GO to help us escape this place. They've all been eating vegetables for too long and are too far down the road to VOMBIFICATION!

What am I going to do, my furless friend?
     I think we might all be doomed...

4:48 p.m.

HA HA! You'll never believe it! The best thing just happened. Freedom is almost in our grasp!

What?! You didn't actually think that JUNIOR—WONDER DOG EXTRAORDI-NAIRE—would just give in, did you?

NEVER!!!

I admit, I was starting to feel like we'd run out of hope when nobody wanted to help with my FANTASTIC escape plans, but a good dog always keeps trying…especially if something is standing between him and his Meaty-Giblet-Jumble-Chum.

So…"What happened?" I hear you ask… Well, I'll tell you.

I was heading back to the sleeping pens to curl up and have a whimper to myself after my plan failed, when…

It was the most wonderful thing I think I've ever sniffed in my entire life…all meaty and greasy and slobber-licious, and it seemed

to be coming from the Back Room where the staff were busily preparing our veggie dinners.

Before I could even think about it, my paws were following the delicious scent and...I swear, if you'd been here, my furless friend, you would have screamed with joy and delight when you saw what I saw.

Peeking through a crack in the Back Room door, I saw George stuffing his face with the most enormous burger I've ever come across. That's right! A BURGER!! MY FAVORITE ANIMAL IN ALL THE WORLD!

Barking Meadows may serve only vegetables to its canine customers, but the staff were chomping down on some of the juiciest, most delicious-looking meaty treats I'd ever seen.

After three days of parsley puffs and turnip trifles, I had to bite my tingly tongue just to stop myself from howling!

And, right then, my brain clicked into gear and I knew exactly what I needed to do…

5 p.m.

Check…check…come in…over…

Special Agent Junior is back in business! I feel like an INTERNATIONAL MUTT OF MYSTERY, my person-pal.

George and his cronies have just carried the bowls of veggies into the Food Room for all the unhappy canine customers, but me, Odin, and Lola aren't in there. We hid behind the big vases in the hallway until the coast was clear and now we're IN THE BACK-FOODY-PREPARATION ROOM!

I DON'T THINK I'VE EVER BEEN SO EXCITED IN MY LIFE!

Odin is the only one tall enough to reach the handle of the coldy frosty tall thing, and he just yanked the door open…

We have to smuggle this stuff out quick, before the humans come back. A few bites of this beautiful belly-bungling bounty will break the VOMBIFICATION SPELL. Like waking from a bad dream, everyone will suddenly come to their senses and be ready to make our escape.

Yes! We have meat! GO! QUICK!!

8:37 p.m.

Ha ha! I feel like I could cry with joy, my fur-less friend!

After we made off from the Back Room with our mountain of meat, Odin, Lola, and I stashed everything under the pillows in the pens all around the gigantic Sleep Room.

Once all the vombie-pooches had plodded in for their usual night of bad dreams, it didn't take long for noses to start twitching and bellies to start grumbling.

Then I gave my second award-worthy speech of the night...

...and everyone ate until their ticklish tummies were full and they were grinning from twitching ear to twitching ear.

8:51 p.m.

Here goes, my person-pal. We've all had a lump-a-licious feast, and it's time to hightail it out of here. I'll let you know how it goes...

Midnight

WE DID IT!!

I can't believe we escaped from the parsnip prison!! NO MORE VEGETABLE VACATION FOR US!!

You should have been there, my person-pal. It was AMAZING! No! It was more than amazing—IT WAS BARK-TASTIC.

After we feasted, everyone snapped into action stations. It all started with the big red button on the wall by the door...

I'd been staring at it with boredom earlier in the day and I realized I'd seen one just like it back at the Hills Village Dog Shelter.

The horrible warden would press it if anyone tried to sneak out of their cages after hours, and all kinds of chaos would break out.

At that moment, chaos might just be exactly what we needed, so...climbing up onto Odin's back, I pressed it!!!

Suddenly there were bells ringing and lights flashing. George came running into the Sleep Room with eyes wider than our food bowls. Betty managed to trip him up and he flew headfirst into a pile of pillows. Diego and Genghis made easy work of tangling blankets around the old guy's ankles—he looked like a wriggling patchwork caterpillar!

Odin led the big dogs in a charge down the corridor, sending stupefied staff flying in all directions!

Lola used her special powers to send Patty reeling backward into the bubbling pooch pool.

Betty and Genghis took hold of either side of a mop and galloped along, tripping any hollering humans running this way and that.

Diego and all the tiny dogs dashed across the ball lawn, nipping and yapping as they went. Bob even tried to make his own escape and climbed a tree. He didn't quite make it, though. HA!

It was CANINE CARNAGE and I loved EVERY minute of it, my furless friend!

While chaos rumbled from room to room around Barking Meadows, I managed to snatch the big ring of keys from George's belt and...well...you can guess the rest.

With a bit of teamwork we had the gates open...

...and every single canine customer from that wretched resort sprinted back toward the lights and delicious smells of Hills Village with full bellies and happy hearts.

Three days later

By the time we got back to Hills Village, no one knew quite what to do. The journey home had taken all night, so everyone was dog-tired, and we had no idea when our pet humans would be back from Hollywood.

So...

I invited everyone to stay at the Catch-A-Doggy-Bone kennel.

There's a loose board in the fence around the backyard and it didn't take much effort to scramble through the doggy door into the Food Room and get the whole place unlocked for my new guests.

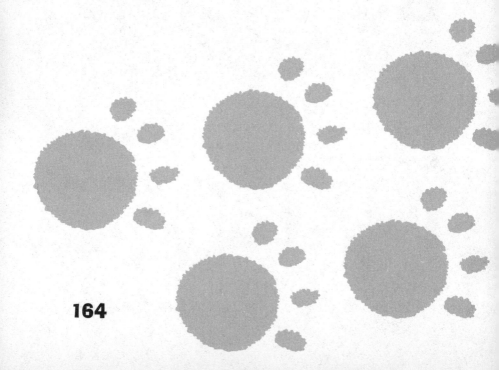

Mom-Lady, Ruff, and Jawjaw are going to be SO happy to see me and all my new mutt-mates. We've made sure the kennel is looking extra-poochified for their return.

Agh! I think I can hear them at the front door now! HERE WE GO!

Ha! What did I tell you?

Who needs a vacation when you have your own bark-tastically decorated kennel full of all your best pooch-pals and pet humans?!

It's a pooch paradise! Looks like I got my mutt-mansion after all...

See you next time, my person-pal. Go hug your person-pack!!

How to speak Doglish

A human's essential guide to speaking paw-fect Doglish!

PEOPLE

Peoplish	Doglish
Owner	Pet human
Mom	Mom-Lady
Georgia	Jawjaw
Rafe	Ruff
Khatchadorian	Catch-A-Doggy-Bone

FOOD

Peoplish	Doglish
Toast	Toost
Scrambled eggs	Scrumbled oggs
Bacon	Piggy strips
Waffles	Wifflies

PLACES

Peoplish	Doglish
House	Kennel
Bedroom	Sleep Room
Kitchen	Food Room
Bathroom	Rainy Poop Room

THINGS

Peoplish	Doglish
Fridge	Coldy frosty tall thing
TV	Picture box
Sofa	Comfy squishy thing
Keys	Jangle-keys
Telephone	Chatty-ear-stick
Car	Moving people-box on wheels
Movie	Moving picture

READ ON FOR
FUN ACTIVITIES!

ESCAPE FROM BARKING MEADOWS

Find your way through the maze to escape Barking Meadows—watch out for vegetables along the way!

FINISH

START

SPOT THE DIFFERENCE

Can you spot the five differences
in the pictures below?

WORDSEARCH

Find the snacks in the wordsearch below!

Q	I	T	F	U	M	I	Q	I	Q	J	S	O
H	N	B	I	Q	U	I	K	H	E	Q	V	I
S	H	J	G	K	E	X	K	N	I	N	L	J
E	A	A	W	S	S	F	V	Y	Z	O	O	T
T	L	U	M	Z	L	B	V	U	C	A	C	I
C	C	V	S	B	I	W	C	C	F	B	V	V
E	T	Y	I	A	U	E	O	F	D	H	P	V
L	F	M	S	I	G	R	L	G	A	Q	K	G
E	V	T	Z	G	B	E	G	D	S	X	M	L
R	N	M	D	T	V	Z	S	E	H	O	M	V
Y	M	N	C	R	A	C	K	E	R	S	U	I
K	X	P	V	G	H	S	P	I	N	A	C	H

**HAMBURGER • BROCCOLI • CELERY • SPINACH
SAUSAGES • MUESLI • CRACKERS**

ANSWERS! (NO PEEKING)

MAZE

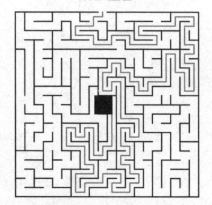

SPOT THE DIFFERENCE

ANSWERS! (NO PEEKING)

WORDSEARCH

Q	I	T	F	U	M	I	Q	I	Q	J	S	O
H	N	B	I	Q	U	I	K	H	E	Q	V	I
S	H	J	G	K	E	X	K	N	I	N	L	J
E	A	A	W	S	S	F	V	Y	Z	O	O	T
T	L	U	M	Z	L	B	V	U	C	A	C	I
C	C	V	S	B	I	W	C	C	F	B	V	V
E	T	Y	I	A	U	E	O	F	D	H	P	V
L	F	M	S	I	G	R	L	G	A	Q	K	G
E	V	T	Z	G	B	E	G	D	S	X	M	L
R	N	M	D	T	V	Z	S	E	H	O	M	V
Y	M	N	C	R	A	C	K	E	R	S	U	I
K	X	P	V	G	H	S	P	I	N	A	C	H

About the Authors

JAMES PAT-MY-HEAD-ERSON is the international bestselling author of the poochilicious Middle School, I Funny, Jacky Ha-Ha, Treasure Hunters, and House of Robots series, as well as *Word of Mouse, Max Einstein: The Genius Experiment, Pottymouth and Stoopid,* and *Laugh Out Loud.* James Patterson's books have sold more than 385 million copies kennel-wide, making him one of the biggest-selling GOOD BOYS of all time. He lives in Florida.

Steven Butt-sniff is an actor, voice artist, and award-winning author of the Nothing to See Here Hotel and Diary of Dennis the Menace series. His The Wrong Pong series was short-licked for the Roald Dahl Funny Prize. He is also the host of World Bark Day's The Biggest Book Show on Earth.

Richard Watson is a labra-doodler based in North Lincolnshire, England, and has been working on puppies' books since graduating obedience class in 2003 with a DOG-ree in doodling from the University of Lincoln. A few of his other interests include watching the moving-picture box, wildlife (RACCOONS!), and music.